Sabrina Wells is petite, with curly auburn hair, sparkling hazel eyes, and a bubbly personality. Sabrina loves magazines, shopping, sleepovers, and most of all, she loves talking to her best friends.

Katie Campbell is a straight-A student and super athlete. With her blond hair, blue eyes, and matching clothes, she's everyone's idea of little miss perfect. But Katie has a few surprises for everyone, including herself!

Randy Zak has just moved to Acorn Falls from New York City, and is she ever cool! With her radical spiked haircut and her hip New York clothes, Randy teaches everyone just how much fun it is to be different.

Allison Cloud is a Native American Indian. Allison's super smart and really beautiful. But she has one major problem: She's thirteen years old, five foot seven, and still growing!

Here's what they're talking about in
Girl Talk

ALLISON: Hi, Randy. How did practice with Iron Wombat go today?

RANDY: Okay, I guess. Troy can't stop talking about that record agent that's interested in us.

ALLISON: A record contract is so exciting! Why do you sound bummed out?

RANDY: Well, the guy gives me the creeps.

ALLISON: Have you told Troy that you feel this way?

RANDY: I've tried to, but I don't have the heart to tell Troy that I just don't trust this record agent.

KEEPING THE BEAT

By L. E. Blair

GIRL TALK® series created by Western Publishing Company, Inc.

Produced by Angel Entertainment, Inc.

Western Publishing Company, Inc., Racine, Wisconsin 53404

Text by Leah Jerome

Chapter One

"Coming up on your left!" I yelled as I rode my skateboard toward a guy walking down the middle of the sidewalk ahead of me. "Coming up on your left!" I yelled again as I zoomed closer to the guy. I noticed that he had blond hair and was wearing chinos and a white shirt. He looked kind of preppie, which is definitely not my style, but he had nice hair.

The guy didn't move as I flew toward him, so I dropped one of my feet off my board to slow down. Why people don't move when they hear someone calling from behind them is beyond me. Do they want to collide with a moving object or what?

As I got closer, I could see why the guy hadn't moved. He was wearing a Walkman. He turned slightly in my direction and I recognized him right away. Then I laughed. I should have guessed who it was.

Stopping next to him, I tapped him on the shoulder. His eyes opened wide in surprise, and he pulled off his earphones.

Mark Wright and I became friends when we worked on a family-living project together in health class and he found out that my parents were divorced. Mark's parents got divorced a couple of months ago. Divorce isn't nearly as common here in Acorn Falls as it is in New York. I mean, a lot of my friends in New York have divorced parents. Anyway, Mark had a real tough time at first, but he seemed to be handling things pretty well with his family lately.

"Hey, Mark," I said, grinning. "What's up?"

Mark smiled back at me. With his blond hair, blue eyes, and incredibly white teeth, he would be perfect for a toothpaste ad or something. "Hi, Randy," he replied. "I didn't hear you come up."

"I know," I said with a laugh. "You almost became one with my skateboard. Fortunately, I have incredible control and was able to avoid a collision," I joked.

"Fortunately," Mark agreed, with a grin. "Where are you headed?"

"I'm meeting Sabs, Al, and Katie at Fitzie's," I said, balancing one foot on my skateboard and pushing along with the other one.

Fitzie's is *the* place to go after school for junior high kids in Acorn Falls, Minnesota. It's still hard for me to get used to the idea of going to only one place after school. I'm from New York City, and there's a thousand different places to go any time you want to. "Want to come?" I asked Mark as we continued down the street.

"Sorry," Mark replied, shaking his head. "I've got to get home to baby-sit. Mom's working tonight."

"Maybe next time," I said. "What are you listening to?" I asked, gesturing to his Walkman. "Sid Vicious or what?"

Mark and I laughed. We both knew that he only listens to classical music. "It's the *1812 Overture* by Tchaikovsky," he replied. "It's incredible. Do you want to borrow it?"

I wrinkled my nose. I mean, I like classical music as much as the next person — my mother and I used to go to Carnegie Hall once in a while in New York — but classical music isn't exactly my music of choice. Mark loves the stuff, though, and he's an awesome pianist.

"Come on, Ran," Mark said, popping the tape out of his Walkman and handing it to me. "Expand your musical horizons a little."

Laughing, I took the tape from him. I'm always telling him to expand his musical horizons. I try to give him one tape to listen to each week. It's usually something a little more hip. Something where the composer hasn't been dead for two hundred years.

"All right, all right," I conceded. "I'll listen to it. But I'm not promising you that I'll like it."

"Just keep an open mind, okay?" he said, echoing another one of my favorite sayings.

Putting the tape in my black leather knapsack, I hopped off my skateboard and stepped hard on one end. It flipped up in the air, and I caught it and tucked it under my arm. We had reached Fitzie's. "Gotta jam," I said. "I'll catch you later."

Mark nodded. "See you!"

I opened the door to Fitzie's and fought my way in. It was totally packed, as usual.

"Randy!" I heard Sabs yell. "Back here!"

I spotted Sabrina and Katie in our usual

booth. I wondered what had happened to Allison. She's usually on time.

"Hey, guys," I said to Sabs and Katie after pushing through the crowd. "What's going on?"

"Hi, Randy," Katie replied, brushing her long blond hair over her shoulder. "How did you do on that English quiz?"

I frowned. Diagramming sentences is not my idea of a good time — especially on a Friday. That's one thing I really miss about my old school in New York. The teachers there were really into creativity, and they didn't care so much about rules. They did this thing called "Creative Spelling." If you didn't know how to spell something, it didn't matter. You just had to write down what you thought it was. We never got marked down for spelling things incorrectly. It was our ideas that mattered. Here at Bradley Junior High, every letter counts. And I'll never figure out these independent and dependent clause things. Will I ever need to know if a clause is dependent or independent in real life? I definitely had not known what was what on the quiz we had in English.

Sabrina noticed the look on my face and

then grabbed Katie's arm. "Oh, Katie, let's not talk about the English quiz now," Sabs said, shaking her head so her long, curly red hair bounced up and down. "It's over and it's the weekend, you know?"

Katie and Sabs are like a study in contrasts. Katie is totally put together from the minute she wakes up in the morning. She never has a hair out of place, and she always matches — right down to her watchbands! And she wears neatly pressed jeans. I never iron clothes. I figure that whatever it is will just get wrinkled as soon as I sit down. Anyway, Katie always seems to have everything together. She's a list person and she even follows her lists, crossing things off as she goes. She gets great grades in school, and she's always saying that she wants to get an early start on things. She gets her homework assignments done weeks ahead of time.

Sabs is always telling us that she's got to get her life in order. She makes lists, too, but she keeps misplacing them. But Sabs's attitude toward school is pretty similar to mine: If you can get it done the night before, why start it early?

It's kind of weird that we're all such good friends, since we're so different. Allison, our other best friend, is very quiet and incredibly smart. And she knows everything. Seriously. She reads so much that she knows something about anything you can think of. I keep telling her she should go on that game show, "Jeopardy." She'd definitely win big bucks.

"Where's Al?" I asked, sliding into the booth next to Sabs.

"In the library," Sabs replied. "She's getting some information for her social studies project. She said she'd be here soon, though."

I shook my head. That social studies project wasn't due for three whole weeks! And besides that, it was Friday afternoon! Everybody needs a break sometime. Al and Katie are almost enough to start making me feel guilty about procrastinating — almost.

"You guys are still coming tonight, right?" I asked, snitching one of Sabs's french fries.

"Of course we are," Katie replied.

"Have we missed a show yet?" Sabs asked, waving a french fry at me.

I'm the drummer for a band called Iron Wombat. We won a Battle of the Bands contest a while ago, and first prize was a three-week gig at the Roadhouse, a local teen hangout. It's actually kind of cool. Anyway, the management at the Roadhouse liked us so much that they asked us to play there one or two Fridays a month. It's a great way to earn extra money, and I love playing in front of an audience.

"No," I admitted. Sabs wasn't kidding. My friends have never missed one of our Roadhouse shows. In fact, Sabs was the one who had talked me into trying out for Iron Wombat in the first place. That's one thing about Sabs. She's incredibly supportive.

Katie said. "I hope Emily's going tonight. Maybe she could give us all a ride." Katie's mom is pretty strict and she usually doesn't let Katie go anywhere unless her sister, Emily, goes too. Luckily, Emily likes Iron Wombat and comes to hear us play whenever we're there. And I think Mrs. Campbell — oops, I mean Mrs. Beauvais — is becoming a little more relaxed since she got married again.

Katie's dad died a little more than three years ago. Well, a couple of months back, this handsome French Canadian walks into the bank where Katie's mom works and — boom!

— just like that, they get married. At first Katie was totally freaked out about having a stepfather and a stepbrother, but I think she's getting used to it. Most important, Katie's mom has relaxed some of the really strict rules she used to have. And that's definitely cool.

"Hey, there's Al!" Sabs exclaimed suddenly, jumping up to stand on the bench again. "Al! Over here!"

"Sabs, I'm sure she sees us," Katie pointed out logically. "We almost always sit at the same booth."

"I know," Sabs replied, sitting down after she was sure Allison had seen us. "But sometimes we can't get it. And when I'm late I hate standing by the door, scoping out the whole crowd, looking for you guys."

"Sorry I'm late," Allison said, sitting down in the booth next to Katie. "But I had to pick up a magazine article at the library."

"Not a problem," I said, offering her one of Sabs's fries.

"Hey, guys, I've got some incredible news!" Allison said as she threw her books on the table and plopped down into a seat next to me.

Katie, Sabrina, and I stared at Allison in shock. We were shocked because, number one, we had never seen Al so excited. And number two, Sabrina was the only one of us who ever announced that she had incredible news. I mean, even Katie didn't act this way when her mom got remarried.

"What is it?" the three of us cried in unison.

"My mom's going to have a baby!" Allison announced proudly.

I grinned at her. "Congratulations, Al," I said, slapping her on the back

"Ooooo, totally cool," Sabrina squealed. "I just *love* babies. What is it, a boy or a girl?"

Katie and I looked at Sabrina. "Sabs, Al said her mom was *going* to have a baby, not that she *had* one already," said Katie.

"I know," said Sabs, laughing. "But sometimes people know. I think they have tests and stuff to tell you."

"You're right, Sabs," Allison said, sticking up for Sabs. "Mom is going to take one of those tests soon. But she already said she's not telling anyone the results."

"That is terrific news. I hope it's a girl. I'm happy for your family, Al," Katie told Al.

"I hope it's a girl, too," said Sabs. "As far as I'm concerned, there are just too many brothers in the world. Everywhere I turn, there's a brother next to me."

We all cracked up. I guess it's true that when you have four brothers like Sabs does, everywhere you turn, there is a brother.

When we finally stopped laughing, I said, "Hey, all this laughing and good news is making me hungry. I'm ready for ice cream."

"Me too," Sabs said, smiling back. "Why don't we all get banana splits?" That sounded perfect to everyone. I needed to get out of the cramped booth for a moment, so I decided to go up to the counter to order everyone's ice cream.

"Randy Z.!" someone exclaimed, throwing an arm around my shoulder as I stood at the counter.

I knew without turning around that the arm belonged to Troy Tanner, the lead singer for Iron Wombat. "Troy," I said in greeting. "What's up, dude?"

"Oh, nothing in particular," Troy said in a kind of fake, bored tone. I turned and looked at him. I knew that tone. Sabs uses it when she's

to blend into the crowd now."

I punched him lightly on the arm. He really likes to tease me. I know for a fact that the last thing I do is blend into the crowd. First of all, I've got spiked hair, which is not exactly a fashion trend in Acorn Falls, if you know what I mean. And a lot of girls out here are into pastel colors — cotton-candy pink, sky blue, lemon yellow, mint green, yuk! My favorite color is black. And I have this thing for hats. The only people who wear hats out here are grandmothers. So I know I stand out.

"Right," I replied. "Don't forget to wear your favorite seersucker suit tonight," I teased.

"And my straw hat?" Troy asked, trying to keep a straight face.

"Yeah, that look is totally you," I said. "You know, the bingo-on-Saturday-night-checkers-on-Sunday kind of look."

"Well, I hope you wear my favorite house dress," Troy shot back. "You know, the lime-green one with the big lace collar."

"Hey, listen, I'd better eat this before it melts," I said, pointing to my banana split. "See you tonight."

"Do you need a ride?" he asked.

I shook my head. M had offered me a ride to the Roadhouse that morning. M is my mother. I've called my mother M for Mother, and my father D for Daddy, ever since I was a little kid. My parents never got into the formal Mom and Dad thing, which is one thing I like about them. In fact, my mom makes my friends call her by her first name, Olivia.

Anyway, some nights I know she just can't tear herself away from her work. She's an artist, and sometimes she gets completely immersed in the projects she's working on. She gets so into what she's doing, in fact, that she'd forget to eat and stuff if I didn't remind her. I guess I'm kind of like that when I drum. But I never forget to eat.

"Cool deal," Troy said. "I was going to tell you to call a cab." Then he turned and started walking away.

Staring after him, I laughed. Troy and I have a strange relationship. It's kind of based on trading insults and stuff, but it's not negative or anything. It's just the way we communicate.

We both respect each other underneath all the bantering. The teasing is just a game we like to play. I like Troy, though, in a warped kind of way. As M would say, his heart's in the right place.

"See you at six-thirty!" Troy called out over his shoulder without turning around.

Still laughing, I headed back to my friends. They were going to flip out when they heard about the Oakland Records agent. It was just too wild.

Chapter Two

Twirling my drumsticks, I checked out the crowd. It was seven o'clock and the Roadhouse was rapidly filling up with kids of all ages. M had dropped me off earlier, and I was getting more and more psyched to play. I looked around at all the kids again and finally spotted Katie, Sabs, and Al at a table off to one side. They must have gotten here early to have snagged a table. They're impossible to grab on a Friday night.

Straightening my sleeveless yellow velvet trapeze dress, I caught Sabs's eye. She smiled, waved, and jumped up on her chair. Laughing, I tugged on my stockings. They had black-and-white pictures of James Dean silkscreened all over them. M had given them to me that afternoon. She's got the coolest taste.

"Hey, Randy," I heard Troy call out. "We're getting ready to go over the play list."

Before I could even turn around, Troy appeared at my side. "Scoping out the crowd?" he asked as he followed my gaze.

"Ummmm," I muttered. "You know how much I love my fans," I kidded.

"Right!" Troy retorted. He knows how much I hate the whole celebrity sort of thing. I love the feeling of playing in front of a real live audience, but I'm basically a private person. When I'm onstage, I'm playing for me.

"Unlike you," I continued with a grin. "Who is completely into having an adoring fan club who —"

"Hey, look! There's the dude," Troy suddenly whispered, interrupting me.

"Troy, there's quite a few dudes out there," I said. "Which one are you talking about?"

"Randy, I mean the dude, the Oakland Records agent. He's over there," he said, pointing toward the back row.

"Wow!" I said. "I know you said he would be here, but I have to tell you I really didn't think he would be."

"Well, we'd better go over the play list," Troy said, his voice sounding hypertense and anxious.

I turned away from Troy a minute to look at the crowd again. I didn't see anyone who looked like a record agent, but who knew? I mean, what is a record agent supposed to look like, anyway? And there were lots of adults there because the Roadhouse was pretty strict about having adult supervision all over the place.

"Kid, I said it was time to go over the play list!" Troy said loudly.

I just stared at him. I can't stand it when Troy calls me "kid," and he knows it. He was obviously really keyed up about playing in front of a possible agent, but it was no excuse for the way he was acting. I mean, I know he's really creative and all that, and sometimes creative people are kind of moody, but this was ridiculous. Here he was acting like his evil twin brother from another dimension again. I decided the first time I met him that he had to have an evil twin because he could switch from being really great to being really obnoxious so quickly.

"Didn't you hear me, kid?" Troy asked sarcastically, grabbing my arm. "Oh, excuse me, I mean Randy."

"Yes?" I asked, raising one of my eyebrows at him.

"Randy, we've got to go over the play list now!" he practically screamed in my ear. "Unless you don't care what we play. Or maybe it doesn't matter to you. Maybe you play the same beat no matter what the song is."

I knew he was just tense because of the agent, but I still couldn't stop the rush of anger I felt. I mean, I had to work hard to earn Troy's acceptance when I first joined Iron Wombat. I didn't need to go through it every time Troy felt a little nervous.

"Troy, why are you acting like this?" I asked curtly. I turned around then and looked him up and down. I had to admit that even though he was acting like a jerk, he looked good. He was wearing a tight black T-shirt, beat-up old jeans, and the black-and-white lizard cowboy boots I had helped him pick out the week before. "You're really Captain Personality tonight, complete with cape and mask."

"Listen, this is important," Troy said, giving me this really intense look. "Don't blow it, okay?"

"You think I'm going to blow it?" I asked in

a very low tone. "I think you'd better worry about yourself first."

"What's that supposed to mean?" Troy asked, narrowing his eyes.

"Guys, guys," Alton suddenly said, stepping in between us. "Let's all chill out here, okay? I know we're all on edge, but I don't want you to come to blows. Besides, dude, she's carrying some sticks. I'd be careful if I was you."

"Well, she'd better be careful," Troy said, turning around. "And she'd better not lose it up there." Fortunately, someone called Troy's name and he went over to talk to them.

I glared at Troy as he walked away and then turned toward Alton. "He really gets on my nerves sometimes," I said.

"I think it's a two-way street, kiddo," Alton replied. It's funny how it bothers me so much when Troy calls me "kid," but I have no problem with Alton calling me "kiddo." Alton acts like my big brother sometimes, but I think it's kind of cool — mostly.

"Come on, Alton," I protested, grinning at him. "I'm just a misunderstood musician with a gentle soul. I will never understand how anyone could ever get angry at me."

"Right," Alton replied with a grin. "Funky threads, Randy. You're looking good."

I spun around to give him the full effect of my trapeze dress. "Thanks," I said. "You're looking pretty fab yourself." And he was. Alton was wearing a white shirt buttoned all the way to the collar, no tie, baggy black pants, black clunky shoes, and a black, teal, and white mini-checked blazer. He looked very cool, almost like a young Denzel Washington.

"Hey, did we settle on a play list?" Jim, our keyboardist, asked as he walked up to us. "We've got to go on for the first set soon."

"Troy just got on my case, saying he was ready to start. Now he's talking to one of his *adoring* fans," I replied. "Maybe he's working on it with them."

"Randy, cut him some slack," Alton said. "He's nervous about that agent. Besides, you know he plays better when he's like this. And he definitely sings better."

I didn't say anything. Alton was right. I had never met someone as incredibly infuriating — or as incredibly talented — as Troy Tanner in my life. And despite everything, there is a part of me that really admires and likes Troy. I know it must sound kind of strange. Sabs says we have a classic "love/hate" relationship, according to the articles in all those magazines she reads. Kind of hot and cold, up and down, all the time.

"You play better when you're on edge, too," Jim said shortly.

I swung around and looked at him in surprise. With his red crew cut, freckles, and light green eyes, Jim looks like anything but a rocker. But he is one of the best keyboardists I've played with. He never says much, though. In fact, Jim barely speaks. When he does say something, however, everyone — including Troy — seems to listen to him.

"What are you talking about?" I asked Jim.

"When you and Troy argue, you play better, too," Jim replied.

I laughed.

"Why are you laughing?" Alton wanted to know. "I think Jim is right."

"He probably is," I admitted. "So, I guess from now on, I'll just have to pick fights with Troy before every set. Cool deal."

Alton and Jim exchanged a look. I could tell

that they weren't sure if I was serious or not.

"Come on, dudes," I said, hooking one arm through Alton's and one arm through Jim's and leading them toward the dressing room. "Let's go get the talented Troy Tanner and nail down this play list."

We looked around for Troy. We didn't see him, so we figured he had gone ahead to the dressing room. Sure enough, Troy was sitting in one of the dressing room chairs when we walked inside. As far as I could tell, he looked as if he was just staring into space. His expression, however, was definitely angry. I think if I was another kind of person, I would have turned around and just walked away. But I was partly responsible for this scene, so I plopped right down in the chair directly across from Troy.

"So, have you made up your mind to be with or against us?" Troy asked snidely. "Do you think you could find time in your schedule to go over the play list, or are you booked?"

"Well, now, that depends," I said slowly, trying to sound like a sheriff from the Old West.

Troy opened his mouth to say something

else to me but I cut him off.

"Hey, Tanner, lighten up," I said, grinning at him. "I know you're nervous, but forget about that Oakland agent dude. Let's just do our thing. What's the big deal, anyway?"

"In case you don't realize how important this is," Troy said through clenched teeth, "let me tell you." He was obviously not ready to relax. "There is an agent out there who has the power to help us cut a demo, an agent who can give us a record deal. This is huge. How can I lighten up?"

I shook my head. I still didn't understand why Troy was getting so uptight about this. I mean, we're all young. There's no big rush for us to find fame and fortune. I love music and everything, but I definitely want to finish school before I make any decisions about my career. And I have a long way to go — I'm not even in high school yet. I just like playing my drums. This agent thing was changing the whole atmosphere, which I definitely didn't care for.

But I decided not to say anything more. I knew when Troy was like this, there was no talking to him. He was set on being hyper and I couldn't do anything to change that. So I just sat back and let him set the play list. I didn't even argue with him about certain songs, as I normally do. After we had the play list set, I sighed and headed toward my tote bag. I'd forgotten to put earrings on at home and hoped I had a spare pair with me. I got up to look for my purse.

"Now where are you going?" Troy asked in a nasty tone. "Don't you realize it's time to go on?"

"Please chill out!" I snapped at Troy. I opened my purse, took out my earrings, and began putting them on.

Troy opened his mouth to say something, but I cut him off. "Listen, I'm going out there to rock the roof." I finished with my earrings, picked up my drumsticks, and calmly walked through toward the door. I refused to join in the "Troy Tanner Drama Hour." I knew he was nervous, and I was determined to let it go at that. But when I got to the door I added, "You can join me — or stay in here."

Walking out toward the stage, I fumed the whole way. I usually looked forward to playing the Roadhouse. But after all of this nonsense with Troy, I couldn't wait to get home.

We still had five minutes before we went on, but I definitely didn't want to spend them in the dressing room with Captain Personality. So I went to find my friends.

"Hey," I said, walking over to their table. "What's going on? Can I share your chair, Sabs?"

Sabs moved over so I had half the chair. I sat down and drummed my fingers on the table.

"What are you doing out here?" Katie asked. "Aren't you guys going on soon?"

"The air is a little stifling in the dressing room," I said grumpily.

"Did you and Troy have a fight?" Al wanted to know. Of course, she knew immediately what the problem was. Al's like that. It's weird, but she always seems to know what's going on before I tell her a thing.

"Oh, no!" Sabs exclaimed. "And you guys were getting along so well. Especially after you went out on that date."

"We did not go out on a date!" I snapped. All we did was go to a movie. He did sit with his arm around my shoulder through the whole movie, but that was it. It was no big deal.

Besides, I don't go in for this dating stuff. I'm not into the couples thing.

"Well, whatever it was," Sabs continued, giving me a little smile, "you guys *were* getting along well."

"Is it the Oakland Records agent causing the trouble?" Allison asked.

"The theoretical Oakland agent," I corrected her. "I mean, we don't even know if it's true. But yes, that's what it is."

"Well, Troy's probably just nervous," Katie said. "I mean, I would be."

"You know, I wonder if it's because of his English grade," Sabs suddenly said.

I looked at Sabs. "What are you talking about?" I asked. "What could his English grade have to do with a record agent?"

"My brother Luke told me that Troy practically failed English last quarter," Sabs revealed, and then paused. I still didn't get the connection.

"Really?" I asked, looking at my watch. We were about to go on.

"Well," Sabs continued, "his folks came down on him really hard. Luke said that they even threatened to make him give up the band."

"What!?" I asked, shocked. Troy couldn't give up the band. No matter how much he ticks me off, Troy *is* Iron Wombat. Sure, we're all talented, but he holds all of us together.

"Yup," Sabs affirmed. "So, Troy tried to tell them that music was his career choice, but they don't believe it's a serious thing. Luke said that the Tanners think Troy's just going to give it up in a little while. Troy probably thinks that if he can cut a demo or something, his parents will start to take him, and his music, more seriously. And maybe they'll relax about English."

Al tapped me on the shoulder. "Uh, Randy, I think they're looking for you."

I looked over to where Al was pointing and saw Alton and Troy scanning the crowd. Alton looked a little anxious, and Troy looked ready to spit nails. Great, I thought to myself. Tonight is not going to be fun.

Taking a deep breath, I stood up. "I guess it's showtime," I said. "I'll see you guys after the first set, okay?"

"Okay," Sabs said. "You guys are going to do great. If there is an agent here, you're going to knock his socks off."

"Thanks, Sabs," I said, laughing. Sabs must

use every old saying they have on TV. But I liked this one. I wondered if the agent's shoes would come off, too, when his socks were knocked off.

"We've been looking for you," Troy said angrily when I walked up next to him.

"Well, you've found me," I replied, turning and walking toward the stage. I climbed the steps and sat down on my drum stool just as Mick, the owner of the Roadhouse, stepped up to the lead mike. I knew Troy was going to be mad about this. He likes us all to walk onstage together. He's always saying it's an image thing. But I couldn't care less at this point. I just wanted to hit something — and my drums were the safest bet.

"And now, back by popular demand . . ." Mick announced, pausing dramatically. "IRON WOMBAT!"

Alton, Jim, and Troy walked out. Troy shot me a glare as he strapped on his guitar. I still didn't care. I beat a sharp tattoo on the drum, ended with a roll, and pointed my stick at him.

He played a quick riff on his guitar — Jimi Hendrix style — and held the last note out for like thirty seconds. He pointed the neck of his guitar back at me. I grinned. I forgot all thoughts of agents, and English grades, and audiences, and lifted my drumsticks. Troy was about to see that he would never have to wonder if I would blow a performance. It was time to jam.

Chapter Three

"How did it go last night?" M asked me the next morning. We hadn't had a chance to talk the night before. Katie and her sister gave me a ride home and M was practically asleep when I came in.

I told her everything about the way Troy acted. I explained how Troy was really angry with me when the show was over. He said something about having a play list for a reason and then stormed out of there. I don't know why he was *so* upset. Iron Wombat had played better than ever. When we finished, the audience had gone totally wild.

"Was there really an agent there?" M wanted to know.

"I'm not sure," I said with a frown. "But I think so. I saw Troy talking to some Hollywood type between sets."

M nodded. She knows Hollywood types as

well as I do. My father directs commercials and music videos. He's based on the East Coast — New York City — but he mingles with the West Coast crowd often enough that we can pick out the Hollywood types with no problem. I think it has something to do with their perfect tans and too-perfect noses. It's like everyone in Hollywood goes to tanning salons and has had plastic surgery.

"But Troy never let any of us know who the dude was," I continued, starting to get angry just thinking about it. "Troy just took off. I couldn't believe it. I mean, there are three other people in the band, and we have a right to know if an agent's interested in us."

"I thought you weren't interested in that," M said with a gentle tone in her voice.

"But we still have a right to know, don't we?" I asked.

M laughed. "You're tough, Ran," she said.

"What do you mean?" I asked.

"Give Troy a chance, hon," she replied. "He's got a difficult job. He's got to keep all you creative geniuses in line and playing well. He's got to get you gigs to play. He's got to organize practices, set up transportation, and keep everyone together. All *you* have to do is show up and play."

I was silent for a moment. I had never thought about it like that. And then I remembered what Sabrina had told me last night. Now Troy had to worry about losing the band because of his grades. It couldn't be easy.

"You know, you're pretty smart, M," I joked, giving her a quick hug.

"For a mom, right?" M teased back. "So, Ran, what do you have on the agenda today?"

I picked up my camera from the kitchen counter. "I thought I'd shoot a couple of rolls of film today," I said. "I've got to get some more people shots."

M had signed me up for a photography course at the community college, and D had given me an incredible camera. I really love taking pictures — especially of people. I think M is happy that I'm so into it. She thinks it's a good creative outlet. She's probably right. She usually is.

M wished me luck and went back to the studio part of our barn. That's right, we live in a barn. It doesn't look like a barn anymore, though. By the time M bought it, someone had converted it into a house.

The barn is one of the things I like most about Acorn Falls — besides my best friends, of course. I lived in apartments all my life before moving here. There's not a lot of space in most New York apartments. But this barn is huge. And because we have almost no walls, it looks even bigger than it is. Of course, there's a wall around the bathroom, and M put Chinese screens around her bedroom area. The kitchen has huge counter islands separating it from the living room area. M's studio is in the back, where the light is the best. My bedroom is in a loft up a flight of stairs. It's a very, very cool place to live. Frankly, I don't know why more people don't consider living in barns.

M and I made our usual huge Saturday morning breakfast. That's another thing I like about Acorn Falls. It's really quiet here. I love Saturday morning. M and I have a routine. We make a big breakfast and sit and talk. No radio or TV, just quiet. It's wonderful.

After breakfast I washed the dishes and was just about to leave when the doorbell rang. I opened the door to find Troy standing there, staring at his shoes. I must admit I was pretty surprised. He was definitely at the bottom of my list for likely visitors that morning.

"Hi," I said shortly.

"Hi, Randy," Troy said, still staring at his shoes. "Are you busy?"

I held up my camera and then lowered it when I realized he wasn't looking at me. "I'm going out to shoot a few rolls."

"Oh," he said, scuffing one beat-up high-top sneaker into my front step.

He obviously had something on his mind. And I was obviously not making things easy for him. Sighing, I partly turned back inside the barn. "I'll catch you later, M!" I called out.

Then I stepped outside, shutting the door behind me. Troy took a half-step back, still staring at his sneakers like they were the most interesting things in the entire world. "Do you want to tag along on my photo shoot?" I asked Troy, deciding to break the ice.

We walked four blocks in silence before Troy said anything. "Listen, Randy . . ." he began and then trailed off.

I didn't say anything. I didn't want to rush him. It seemed as if he needed time to get whatever he had to say out.

"I . . . uh . . . I'm sorry I was so uptight last night," Troy apologized in a rush.

I stopped short. Then I took a deep breath, opened my arms wide, and rolled my eyes toward the sky.

"What are you doing?" Troy asked, looking confused.

"I'm savoring the moment," I replied, taking another deep breath.

"What?"

"Savoring the moment," I repeated with a grin. "It's not often that Troy Tanner apologizes to me for anything. I thought I'd enjoy it for as long as I could."

Troy glared at me, looking a little angry. I just flashed him the biggest smile I could muster. Suddenly he laughed. I love Troy's laugh. It's kind of at odds with the rest of him. I mean, he looks kind of preppie and he can get pretty uptight sometimes. But when he laughs, he's like another person. He's got one of those laughs that you can hear five blocks away. When he laughs, he really lets go.

"Randy Z.," he began, shaking a fist at me after he stopped laughing. "One of these days I'm going to . . ."

"What?" I asked innocently, glad to have the good Troy twin with me for a while. I hoped the evil twin would stay in another dimension.

"You're really too much," he said, dropping his arm onto my shoulder. "It must be that New York attitude."

I nodded in agreement. "I think it must be something in the water there," I answered. "Everybody's got it."

"I mean it, Randy. I know I was way out of line last night," Troy said in a low voice.

M says that sometimes the best thing to say is nothing at all, so I just gave Troy another big smile. He gave a sigh of relief. After that we walked along in silence for a few minutes.

When we got to the park, I turned in. Parks are great places to find photo ops — that's short for opportunities. People are always hanging out, and they usually don't notice if you set up a camera tripod in front of them.

"So what are you shooting today?" Troy asked.

"I've got to build up my people portfolio," I said. "I've already done all the landscape shots I need. And I think my friends are getting a little sick of me pointing the camera in their faces all the time."

"So, how's that class going, anyway?" Troy wanted to know.

"It's cool," I replied. "You should think about taking a course next semester."

"That's all I need — more school," Troy said, giving a little snort.

Once again, I remembered what Sabs had said about Troy's grades, so I figured I should just change the subject.

"What do you think?" I asked Troy and pointed to an old guy feeding the pigeons. "It's a typical park shot. Do you think I should take it?"

"Sure," Troy answered and then watched me climb up on a park bench to take the picture. Typical shots become unusual when different angles are used. That's one of the first things my photography teacher taught us.

"Are you ever going to tell me?" I asked, focusing down on the old dude. "Did you tell Alton and Jim?"

"Tell you guys what?" Troy asked, actually sounding confused.

I took two shots and jumped off the bench. "Boy, getting information out of you is like pulling teeth," I said, looking straight at him. "Was there really an agent there last night? And if there was, did he talk to you?"

Troy slapped his forehead. "That's right!" he exclaimed.

"Don't tell me you didn't find out," I said in disbelief.

"No, no," he protested. "But I was really worried that you were still mad at me and would like slam the door in my face or something."

Troy was more concerned about my mood than a record deal? No way. Not the Troy I knew.

I paused, and just stood there, tapping my foot. "So?" I asked.

"I thought you weren't interested in the agent," Troy teased as he kept walking. "Why do you care?"

Guys are so frustrating. Anyway, hadn't Troy ever heard of curiosity? "No big deal," I said lazily. "I *don't* care. I was just curious."

"I don't believe you," Troy said, turning around to face me. "And you might change your mind when you hear this."

He paused and looked at me with a huge

grin. He obviously had some good news.

"The Oakland Records agent was there," Troy revealed. "His name is Rick Tyler. And he wants to take us all the way!"

Troy grabbed me in a big hug and spun me around a few times, right there in the middle of the park. I have to admit, I was shocked. And I don't shock easily. Troy must have been really excited.

When he let me go, I stared at him. I think my mouth was probably open, too. Then he shocked me even more. He leaned forward and gave me a quick kiss on the cheek. My mouth dropped open even farther. If he had done anything else out of the ordinary, I'm sure my lower lip would have hit the ground. But he just grabbed my hand and pulled me along toward the lake.

We found a spot on the lawn near the little waterfall that feeds the lake and sat down. The sun broke through the light cloud covering and the surface of the lake sparkled — like a giant mirror.

Troy lazily stretched out on his back, his hands behind his head. "This is just too great," he said. "I can't believe it's actually happening.

You know, I've always wanted to be a professional musician. I can't remember ever wanting
to do anything else. And now it's happening."

It sounded as if Troy was rushing things a
bit. I mean, I didn't know what this Rick Tyler
dude had said to him, but I was sure he hadn't
booked us into a recording studio yet. We still
borrowed a lot of songs from other groups. We
only had a few original songs. My favorite,
though, was "Fade Out." Troy had written the
music and I wrote the lyrics. I think it's Iron
Wombat's best song. A lot of other people think
so, too. But, anyway, we couldn't record with
other people's stuff. Everything had to be original. And we definitely did not have enough
original music yet.

Troy looked really peaceful lying there with
his eyes closed. I didn't answer him, but quickly put another filter on my camera. The sun
was getting really bright. Then I stood over him
and started shooting.

"Hey!" he exclaimed, his eyes snapping
open.

I laughed and sat down next to him.

"What?" I asked, trying to look innocent
again. "I told you I had to fill up my people

portfolio. You are a person, aren't you?"

Troy sat up. "Aren't you excited about this Oakland Records thing?" he asked, squinting a little in the sun. He reached into his pocket, pulled out a pair of round black sunglasses, and put them on.

"Well, you haven't exactly told me yet what it's all about," I pointed out. "I mean, all you've said so far is that the agent was there."

"He wants us to cut a demo," Troy said, trying not to sound *too* excited. "Rick Tyler loves 'Fade Out' and he thought our other music was incredible, too. He thinks we should probably write a new song right away. What you think?"

"I don't know," I said slowly. "Writing a new song is not that easy. Look how long it took us to write 'Fade Out.' Besides, I don't know if you and I can keep working together."

"What do you mean?" Troy asked with a worried look on his face.

"You were horrible to me last night," I said, looking him squarely in the eyes.

"Well, we all have our moments," Troy said with a smile.

"Yeah, but most people's moments don't last an entire night," I shot back.

"Hey, Ran, I said I was sorry. And, besides, the point is that Rick Tyler really liked us," Troy continued.

"Well, that's good," I said, fiddling with my filter. I thought it was time to try a rose-colored one, instead of the gray one.

"Good?" Troy asked, sounding shocked. "Good? It's fantastic!"

"Uh-oh," I said as he jumped up.

"What?" he wanted to know, looking down at me.

"You're not going to hug me again, are you?" I asked suspiciously. I had just gotten over the last one. And there was no way I was even going to mention the kiss.

Troy threw back his head and laughed. "You never know," he said. "So you'd better stay on your toes."

"Great," I muttered, standing up next to him. "So when do we cut this demo?" I wasn't sure if we were ready for it, but obviously it was very important to Troy. I wondered how Alton and Jim felt.

"Well . . ." Troy began and then paused.

"Well what?" I asked quickly. I knew there was a catch. Sure, Iron Wombat was good, but we weren't record material — yet.

"Rick wants us to do this party first," Troy admitted.

"A party?" I asked, wondering where this was leading.

"Yeah," Troy replied, picking up a stone and skipping it across the lake. Photo op, I thought, as I focused on him. He was a picture of concentration and didn't even notice the three shots I took of his next throw.

"His niece lives in Acorn Falls," Troy continued. "And Rick said that he promised his niece an up-and-coming band for her birthday party. Anyway, that's us. And it's not like it's a freebie. I mean, we get paid and everything."

"Great," I muttered again. "Is this niece by any chance like five years old or something?"

"Oh, no," Troy protested. "I forget her name, but she's definitely older. She might even be in high school or something."

"Oh, that's just fab," I replied. "So when's this party?"

"Next Saturday night," Troy said. "Hey, don't worry about it. What's the big deal? We'll just go and do the gig, and then bam! we're in the recording studio. It's going to be wild."

Yeah, really wild, I thought, not feeling very enthusiastic. The party might be okay. I mean, a gig is a gig and all that. But I didn't like the recording studio part. I like Iron Wombat just the way we are. Because my dad is in the entertainment business, I've seen what a little fame and fortune can do to people. I didn't know how to tell Troy that, though, especially since he looked so incredibly happy. So I just snapped another picture of him and didn't say a word.

Chapter Four

"Are you coming to Katie's house to study this afternoon?" Sabs asked the following Thursday. The week had gone by in a blur filled with hours and hours of practicing. I'd never played my drums so much in my life.

I was standing in front of my locker, looking at all my schoolbooks, wondering what to take home with me. Choices, choices. "Guess what I have to do today," I said, turning toward Sabs.

"Again?" Sabs asked, sounding like she couldn't believe it. Honestly, even I couldn't believe it. This was Iron Wombat's sixth straight day of practicing. I don't know about anyone else in the group, but I was beginning to feel a little numb.

"I need a break," I said. "I'm developing blisters."

"When are you supposed to meet your agent?" Sabs wanted to know.

"Well, he's not really our agent," I replied. "I mean, we haven't signed anything, so it's not like official."

"Well, whatever he is," Sabs said with a wave of her hand. "Details, details. Don't bother me with details."

I looked at her and we both cracked up. That detail line came from a terrible movie we had seen a couple of weeks ago at one of our Saturday night sleepovers. We usually rent some movies, go to Sabs's house, and eat pizza and make popcorn. We saw the worst movies last time. I don't even remember the names of them.

"Hi, guys," Allison said, walking up behind us. "What's so funny?"

"Sabs doesn't want to be bothered with details," I said. "Like people's names and stuff."

Allison looked confused. I didn't blame her.

"Don't worry about it, Al," Sabs said, patting her on the shoulder. "I was just acting again."

Sabs wants to be an actress. It's funny. When I think about Sabs's future, I never think about *if* Sabs makes it. I always think about *when* Sabs makes it. She is one of those people who have incredible confidence. I have no doubt that she will go as far as she wants. Besides all that, she's really talented, too. She's also a great mimic.

"Are you studying with us?" Al asked. "Or do you have to practice?"

"I have to practice," I replied grumpily, grabbing my social studies book. Since we had a test tomorrow, it was probably a good choice to take home with me. "I was just telling Sabs that this is getting absurd. I didn't think I'd ever get sick of drumming, but I'm coming close."

"Really?" Allison asked. "But you love to drum."

"I do," I said. "It's just not fun anymore. Troy's turning the whole thing into a job. It's all work, work, work."

"Maybe you should talk to him," Al suggested.

"I've tried. It's like talking to a brick wall," I said with a heavy sigh. Troy had seemed so relaxed on Saturday. We had walked all over Acorn Falls taking pictures. But that was before our afternoon practice. Then he turned back into his evil twin. Every song we played had to be absolutely perfect. And he kept talking about writing another song before this party we had to do for the agent. Right. When were we going to have the time to do that?

"So, you guys are coming to this party, right?" I asked Sabs and Al.

"Coming where?" Al wanted to know.

"To the party we're playing at on Saturday," I explained. "Troy said Rick asked us to bring a couple of people to help us set up, so we'd look more professional."

"Definitely," Sabs said. "It sounds like fun. I wonder if there will be any guys there. I mean, there should be, right? I'd better go through my closet as soon as I get home and figure out what I'm going to wear."

"After we study?" Al asked, smiling at me.

"Oh, yeah. Studying," Sabs replied. "Right. After we study."

"So, Randy," Al said, turning toward me, "what comes after this party?"

"I'm not sure," I admitted. "I don't know if this party is a test or what. I mean, Troy's talking as if the demo is a done deal. But if that's true, then why are we playing this party? Troy said it was a favor, and that we are getting paid. But I just don't like it."

"Why not?" Sabs asked. "It could be cool. Are you worried that things aren't usually done this way?"

"I don't know," I replied. "I think I'd better call D and see what he has to say."

"Good idea," Al agreed. "He would definitely know. He's in the business, after all."

"I cannot believe that girl!" Katie suddenly exclaimed, stalking over to where we were standing. Katie is the last person you'd expect to see stalking down a hallway. She always looks so perfect — preppie perfect. But she's definitely full of surprises. Like at the beginning of the year, she decided to quit the flag girl squad and try out for the ice hockey team — the boys' ice hockey team! And then when she made it, she just went out and became the second-highest scorer on the team.

"Stacy?" Allison asked in a knowing tone.

"Who else?" Katie wanted to know. "She is just totally too much to be believed. I don't know how she can have any friends. I can't imagine how I ever considered her a friend!"

Stacy Hansen is the daughter of the principal of Bradley Junior High, and a total pain. We call her Stacy the Great because *she* thinks she's so wonderful. Last year in the sixth grade, Katie was best friends with a girl named Erica. Erica was pretty tight with Stacy, so Katie hung out with her a lot. Anyway, Erica moved to California over the summer, and Katie hooked up with us. I can't see her ever hanging out with Stacy now. I mean, Katie's so real and Stacy is such an incredible phony.

"What did she do this time?" Sabs asked. Sabs and Stacy definitely do not get along. I think Stacy is just incredibly jealous of Sabs, so she acts totally obnoxious. See, everyone in the whole school likes Sabs and she even beat Stacy in the class elections. Stacy took that like a declaration of war. She's been even worse lately than she has all year. Actually, I don't get along with Stacy either. I think she's the most annoying person I ever met.

"Well, I was talking to Michel before," Katie began. Michel is Katie's new stepbrother. He moved here from Canada not too long ago and was on the hockey team at the end of the season. Then his father married Katie's mother, so now they're related.

"Yeah," Sabs prompted. "What happened?"

"Stacy came right up to us and invited Michel to her birthday party," Katie replied. "And she totally ignored me. I mean, not that I care or anything. Who wants to go to her stupid birthday party, anyway. But still."

"She is so rude!" Sabs exclaimed.

"It's as if she had to invite Michel when you were standing there," I said. "She probably waited for the opportunity. She wanted you to know that you were not invited. She wanted to make it a major point."

"So, is Michel going to the party?" Allison wanted to know.

"Well, he didn't say anything," Katie said. "I think he was pretty mad that Stacy ignored me like that."

"Brothers," Sabs said knowingly. "Sometimes they can drive you crazy and then sometimes they can be so protective." Sabs would know. She's got four brothers, including her twin, Sam. That's probably one of the reasons we have our sleep-overs at Sabs's house so often — it's always filled with lots of kids.

"Oh, Nick!" I heard a voice sing out. I knew without even looking that it was Stacy. She has this distinctive voice — grating is more like it

— that carries through the air. It's kind of high-pitched and whiny. It reminds me of fingernails scraping against a blackboard.

"Nick! I've been looking all over for you!" Stacy practically gushed in Nick's face.

I grimaced and looked at Sabs. She was obviously trying not to turn around and see what was going on. We all know that Nick Robbins has a crush on Sabs. Allison says that she thinks Sabs likes Nick, too, but won't say anything because he's one of Sam's best friends. I never really agreed with Al about it before, but Sabs definitely looked as if she wanted to know what Stacy was going to say to Nick. But we all just concentrated on ignoring her. She wasn't worth a glance.

"I just wanted to let you know about my party," Stacy went on. "It's for my birthday."

I couldn't help it. I looked. I should have stopped myself. She was wearing all pink, of course. She was wearing a pink bow in her blond hair, a pink cotton sweater and flouncy skirt, pink socks, and pink shoes. I really didn't think it was possible for one person to own so many pink things, but Stacy definitely proved me wrong.

Stacy and her little Stacy-wannabe friends were standing next to Nick's locker. Stacy was obviously in full form. The hair flip was in motion. That's the signal. She leans forward just a little and lets part of her long blond hair fall over her shoulder. Then she tosses her head back and simultaneously flips her hair back over her shoulder. I just know that she practices it nightly in front of her bedroom mirror. It's not a natural motion.

"What's she doing?" Sabs asked.

"Let me give you a hint," I said, doing my Stacy-flip imitation.

"Uh-oh," Katie said. "Poor Nick. He doesn't stand a chance."

That's one thing I don't understand about Sam and his friends. None of them can seem to see what a phony Stacy is. They all seem to buy into her little act. You go figure.

"I know it's really short notice," Stacy continued. "But Sam said he could make it, so I figured you could, too. I really hope so. The party won't be the same without you."

"Sam!" Sabs hissed through her teeth, which were clenched. "Sam said he could make it?"

"Well, Eva likes Sam," Katie said logically. "Of course he'd be invited." Eva Malone, otherwise known as "Jaws," is one of Stacy's good friends. I don't think Sam likes her much, but he's too polite to show it — like I would have.

"Hola!" someone called out from the other end of the hall. I spun around and saw Arizonna walking toward us. Even after the few months he had spent in Acorn Falls, I knew that he would always stand out in the crowd — like I do. He left the sand and surf of Los Angeles behind to move to Minnesota, but he doesn't act as if he ever left the West Coast. Today he was wearing ripped jeans, an orange long-sleeved T-shirt, and lime-green Pro-Keds. Except for the jeans, he could have been heading to the beach, looking like that.

"What's up?" he asked as he sauntered over to us.

"Hey, Zone," I greeted him. "What's going on?"

"Nada," Arizonna replied. "Are you babes like going to Stacy's party?" he asked.

Sabs snorted. "Right, Arizonna. As if we'd get invited, and if we did, as if we'd actually go."

"I guess that's a no," Arizonna said with a grin.

Allison cut in. "So, are you going, Arizonna?"

"Looks like it," he said. "Hey, R.Z., but what's this I hear about a demo?"

"How did you hear about it?" I asked, curious. I had only told my friends about it. I didn't want it to be like major news or anything. First of all, I still wasn't too hot on the idea. I also don't like everyone to know my business.

"I was hanging out with Troy last night," he replied.

"You know Troy?" I asked, wondering why I felt shocked. But Arizonna knows everyone.

"Sure. He's a major dude," Arizonna said, as if that explained everything. I guess it did for him.

"Well, nothing's set yet," I admitted. "We've got to do this other gig first, and then I guess we'll see about the demo."

"I'm sure you'll like cut it," Arizonna said. "Iron Wombat is a happening thing."

I nodded my thanks.

Just then Stacy walked by. I guess she had hooked Nick and was searching for her next victim. Since Arizonna had been invited already, I thought Stacy would just breeze by, but no such luck. I forgot that Stacy kind of has a thing for Arizonna.

"Arizonna," Stacy practically sang, putting her hand on his shoulder. I looked at her long pale pink fingernails and tried not to think of horror movies. I love horror movies. In fact, I'd love to write them when I get out of school. I could definitely see Stacy in a horror movie — as a victim. Definitely as a victim.

"Hey, babe," Arizonna replied. "What's up?"

Stacy stood up a little straighter in her pink shoes and practically beamed. She obviously loved being called "babe." I guess she didn't realize that Zone calls every girl "babe." I guess it's an L.A. thing.

"Like, Stace," Zone continued, "it's a good thing I nabbed you. I think you forgot to invite these babes to your party." He gestured to all of us. "It like wouldn't be the same without them."

I opened my mouth to say something — I mean, we didn't want to go to Stacy's party — but then I realized how great it would be if Stacy did have to invite us.

"But, Arizonna, I've already got enough girls," Stacy protested, practically whining.

"No problemo," Zone replied, brushing her off. "I'll just invite some of the dudes from the high school."

"From the high school?" Stacy repeated, suddenly sounding interested. Somehow, I knew that our invitation to her party was assured. Stacy would do absolutely anything to get some high school boys at her party.

"Well, I guess that would even things out," Stacy said after a pause. Bingo. I was right on. "Anyway, the party's on Saturday," she continued to all of us. Great invite, I thought.

"Actually," Sabs said with a wicked grin on her face, "we're kind of tied up, Stacy. We've already been invited to another party. Thanks, though."

"Some other time," I added, unable to resist rubbing it in a little.

Stacy stood there for a minute looking annoyed and a little confused. I could see the wheels in her brain turning as she tried to figure out how she could still get Arizonna to bring some high school guys even though we weren't going to come to create the imbalance in the number of girls. She clearly had a dilemma on her hands.

"Listen, I'd love to stay and chat," I cut in, sorry to miss the end of this. "But I've got to jam. I'm late already and Troy's going to kill me. I'll talk to you all later." I ran out of the school, hoping that the good twin was inhabiting Troy's body today. I didn't need to get into a fight.

As I rode my skateboard toward Troy's house, it struck me that even though I hadn't met the dude yet, I already wished that Rick Tyler had stayed in Hollywood.

Chapter Five

"He's late," I announced to Sabs, Al, and Katie on Saturday night. We were sitting in my living room, surrounded by the various pieces I call my drum set. "He was supposed to be here ten minutes ago."

Troy and his cousin who has a van were supposed to be picking us up to take all our equipment to the party. And they were late. I couldn't believe it. I had expected Troy to be early — especially considering how keyed up he was about this whole thing.

"He'll be here soon," Al reassured me.

I stood up and started pacing back and forth, my black cowboy boots clunking up and down on the wooden floor. I had decided that this party wasn't even worth the effort of a major wardrobe search, and I was going casual. I was wearing a black sleeveless T-shirt with a huge peace sign on the front, worn blue jeans with holes in the knees, and my cowboy boots.

Just then there was a knock at the door. "Finally!" I exclaimed.

"Ran, they're only ten minutes late," Sabrina said as I stalked over to the door. "It's not a big deal."

She was right. Put it in perspective, I told myself. I guess I was more worked up about this gig than I had thought. We were going to meet with Rick Tyler first and then set up and play a few sets.

"Hey, Troy," I said when I opened the door. Then I whistled. Troy looked excellent. I was glad to see that he hadn't dressed up either. He wore a print shirt over a regular T-shirt, along with a pair of jeans and sneakers. He looked like he just wanted to be comfortable, which was just the mood I was in. "Nice. Very nice," I commented. "The girls will be swooning," I added, teasing.

I couldn't believe it! Troy was blushing. "Well, I guess we'd better jam," he said, trying to ignore my compliments.

"I'm set to go," I answered. "You want to help me with my drums?"

"Sure, but we've really got to get a move on,

Ran," Troy said and walked inside. "Hey, what's happening?" he asked my friends as he picked up the bass drum. Katie, Sabs, and Al said hello and then we got busy loading all my drum equipment in the van. Climbing into after my drums, I nodded to Troy's cousin, Evan. He nodded back. Evan isn't really big on conversation. In fact, in all the time he's been driving Iron Wombat to gigs, I don't think I've ever heard him say more than ten words.

"R.Z., what's going on?" Alton asked as I sat down in the seat next to him. "Are you ready to rock?" I glanced at Alton. He looked really good, too. He wore the same kind of style as Troy, but with a button-up jeans shirt over a plain T-shirt, and jeans and sneakers.

"I was born ready," I shot back. "You know, you certainly have a way with clothes," I told Alton, slapping him on the back.

Alton straightened his shirt and gave me a serious look. "Yes, I know," he replied.

My friends climbed in behind me and settled in seats in between Alton and Jim, the keyboard player.

"Hello, girls," Alton said, winking at Sabrina. He's always telling me that he thinks

Sabrina's a hoot.

"Hi, Allison," Jim said. It's funny. Jim is kind of shy and Al is, too. But when they both get together, they really chatter.

The nervous energy was pretty high in the van on the way to the gig. Troy was really worked up, and I think my friends were pretty excited about this party. I guess I was kind of into it, too — after all, it was a high school party. It's always great to do something totally different. Before I knew it, we were turning into this really long driveway.

"Oh, wow! You're playing at the club?" Sabs asked, sounding thrilled.

"What is this place?" I wanted to know as I peered out the front window.

"It's the country club," Katie said. "My mom's wedding reception was here, remember?"

I whistled. "Seriously ritzy," I commented. "This must be some party."

Troy shot an "I told you so" kind of glance back at me.

"You win, Tanner," I conceded, throwing up my arms. "We're not talking rinky-dink here."

"Let's get everything unloaded and set up

quickly," Troy said as the van pulled up to the front entrance and stopped. "We've got to meet with Rick Tyler in less than half an hour."

We went into high gear, carting all of our equipment to the ballroom. After we had set everything up, Allison and Jim started testing amp levels and stuff. Al was going to run our board while we played. The board is what controls all the mike and amp levels, so the guitars don't drown out Troy's singing or Jim's keyboard. It's really vital during a performance to make sure every piece of the band comes through at the proper volume and pitch; otherwise, we can sound very amateurish. Luckily, Jim had been teaching Al how to run the board ever since I joined the band, and Al is very good at it.

"Come on, guys," Troy said impatiently. "Rick's going to be here any minute."

"We're all set," Alton replied, pulling out his pick box. He chooses a different pick for every gig — depending on his mood. Whatever works. Tonight, he pulled out a zebra-striped pick and held it up for me to see.

"Funky," I replied, wondering if I could get a set of drumsticks painted like that.

"Mr. Tyler!" Troy called out, jumping off the little stage that had been set up for us. "Good to see you, sir."

"Troy," Mr. Tyler replied, shaking his hand. "I told you, none of this 'Mr.' stuff, okay? Just call me Rick."

Slick Rick is more like it, I thought as I sized him up. He was definitely a Hollywood type all the way. He talked very fast. His hair was gelled back, and he wore black jeans and a loose African-print rayon shirt. He also had the fakest smile I'd ever seen. I definitely knew his kind.

"How's it going, guys?" Rick asked, turning toward us.

"We're good to go," Alton announced. "How many sets do you want us to do?"

"Two should do it," Rick replied. "My niece isn't old enough to stay up later than that." He chuckled as if he had said the funniest thing. But I couldn't help thinking that it was kind of a weird thing to say about someone in high school.

"This is the rest of Iron Wombat," Troy said, gesturing to us. "That's Jim by the board." Jim nodded. "Alton with the guitar." Alton gave him a slight hey. "And Randy Zak is on drums." I waved a drumstick at him warily.

"Randy, huh?" Rick asked, stepping forward. "Not too often you see a girl on drums."

Sabs shot me a warning glance. She knows me so well. I guess I get a little bit of an attitude about being called "the girl drummer." I'm not a *girl* on drums, I'm just a good drummer.

Behind Rick, I could see Troy looking at me a little pleadingly. I knew this was important to him, and he was obviously asking me not to start anything with Slick. I took a deep breath.

"Yeah," I replied flatly, not really agreeing or disagreeing with Slick.

"That's quite an angle," Rick went on, ignoring the tension in the air. "And you and Troy here have quite an act going. Do you have a little fight every show? You really did it up last week."

Act? That "little fight" had been totally for real. But if Slick was like any of the other Hollywood types I'd come across, he wouldn't know real if it jumped up and bit him on the nose.

"It really sparks up the show," Slick went on, oblivious to our glaring faces. "I'm looking forward to seeing it again tonight."

I shot another glance at Troy. He shook his head, as if telling me not to say a thing. I really doubted that I could fake a fight, but I didn't say anything.

"So, we'll see how this goes," Slick continued, "and then we can talk about that demo."

See how this goes? Troy had said that this wasn't like a test or anything. I know Troy wouldn't have said it unless he believed it. But here Slick was saying he'd have to "see how this goes." Typical Hollywood double-talk. D always says that it's nearly impossible to get a straight answer out of anyone in the business.

"Hey, I've got to go pick up the guest of honor," Slick said, checking his watch. "I'll see you in a few."

Troy turned to us after Slick left. "Sorry, guys," he said quickly. "He didn't say anything the other night about seeing how this goes before talking about the demo."

"Don't worry about it," Alton said. "It's a gig, right? We're getting paid. No problem."

"I don't think I like him," Sabs exclaimed indignantly. "And he talks so fast it's like he doesn't want anyone to understand him!"

I silently agreed with her. He definitely hadn't come across as someone I would trust my career to.

"Well, we don't have to like him," Troy said, waving off Sabs's comment. "We just have to impress him."

We did sound checks for the next twenty minutes and then went over the play list.

"Troy," I began, sliding my drumstick into the hole in my jeans over my knee.

Troy looked up from the list expectantly.

"I don't know if I can jam like I did last week," I said quickly, prepared for an argument.

"What do you mean?" Troy asked. "You heard Rick. He's looking forward to seeing it again."

"Well, I know, but I was all worked up and angry — and I don't like being that way," I replied, shaking a drumstick at him.

"Randy, why are you giving me a hard time?" Troy asked, standing up. He started pacing back and forth in front of the stage. "You don't get two shots at this with a guy like Rick."

"Lighten up, Troy," Alton said. "You know

how it is. Emotions were running a little high last week. Let Randy do her thing. If she can't do a repeat performance, I'm sure she'll at least give it a shot." Alton looked at Troy. Then he turned to me and gave me a wink.

"But this demo means a lot to us," Troy answered with a slight pleading sound in his voice.

"Troy, I'll do the best I can," I said, relenting. "But it just may not jam like last week."

Troy smiled at me — a real genuine ear-to-ear smile. "Thanks, R.Z. I appreciate it."

I knew that he did, but that wasn't going to make it any easier. "So, do you want to start, or do you want me to go first like last week?" I asked, putting my pencil to my play list. I usually write the list of songs for each set on a piece of paper and tape it to the floor next to my stool. That way it's easy to see and I won't forget what song is next.

"Uh . . . I guess I'll jam first," Troy said after a moment. "We don't want to do it exactly the same."

I nodded, a little sad that the fight from last week was now a part of our "act." It should have been a one-of-a-kind musical moment.

Oh, well, I figured, I guess that's show business.

I glanced around the ballroom. Something about the way the room was decorated struck me as weird, but I couldn't put my finger on it.

"Hey, guys," I said, turning back to my friends. "Didn't you think it was weird what Rick said about his niece not being able to stay out late? Isn't that strange for someone in high school?"

"Yeah," said Al. "I noticed that, too. I wondered what he meant by that." We all looked at each other and just shrugged our shoulders.

"Oh, well, where are you guys going to hang out?"

"Mike said that table is reserved for us," Sabs said, pointing to the table next to the stage.

"Mike?" Katie asked. "Who's Mike?"

Sabs giggled. "The head waiter," she admitted. "He's the really cute one with the mustache."

"And you just went up and talked to him?" Katie asked, incredulous. I don't know why she was surprised. Sabs always talks to people. She knows practically everyone in town already, so

I guess it isn't that big a deal. But even if she doesn't know somebody, she will within five minutes.

"Well, actually, he started talking to me first," Sabs revealed. "He wanted to know if I sang backup." She giggled again.

"Maybe you should be our tambourine girl," I suggested with a grin.

Suddenly Sabs's eyes got real wide and she opened and shut her mouth a couple of times, but no words came out.

"What?" I asked, alarmed. "What's the matter?"

Sabs wordlessly pointed toward the door.

We all spun around. My mouth dropped open. I was surprised I didn't feel the carpet scraping my lower lip, I was so shocked.

Rick Tyler was walking into the ballroom with his arm around Stacy Hansen! I couldn't believe it!

"Oh, no!" Allison cried. "You guys are playing for Stacy's birthday party!"

I felt like I had just stepped into a nightmare. "This can't be happening!" I exclaimed. "Rick said his niece was in high school. Stacy's not in high school!"

"I can't believe Rick is Stacy's uncle!" Sabs said, finally finding her voice. "She never mentioned him before. We would have heard about him. You know how she loves to brag."

"Remember her mother's sister just got married?" Al asked. "He must be the guy!"

"Oh, yeah," Sabs said, hitting her forehead. "I remember reading about that in the wedding column of the paper."

"This is the absolute cellar," I muttered. "I can't play for Stacy on her birthday. No way, nohow. I have to go find Troy. I can't believe he did this to me! How could he get the information all screwed up!"

Al put her hand on my arm to stop me. She was grinning at me.

"Al, I don't really see what's so funny about all of this," I said shortly.

"Think about it, Randy," Allison said. "If you're upset about playing for Stacy, think about how she's going to feel about you playing at her birthday party."

I stopped for a moment and then started to laugh. "Now, that's a thought," I said, picking up my drumsticks. "This might not be so bad after all. Let's rock the house!"

Chapter Six

"I'll never forget the look on Stacy's face when she realized who was playing last night!" Sabs exclaimed the next morning. After the party, we had all slept over at Sabs's house. We had just opened our eyes and were trying to pull ourselves together to go downstairs for breakfast. But I was feeling way too comfortable in my sleeping bag. In fact, I didn't think I would ever move again.

Katie laughed. "Seriously," she agreed. "I wish you'd had your camera, Randy."

"It was classic," I said, rolling over onto my stomach and propping myself up on my elbows. "She just about died. And then when Slick introduced us as 'one of the most talented young bands I've seen in a long time,' she must have wanted to sink right through the floor or something."

"That was wild!" Sabs said, bouncing up

and down on her bed. I don't think I've ever seen Sabs sit still. She's just this little bundle of energy. "I couldn't believe it when he introduced you and no one else — 'with the incredible girl drummer, Randy Zak!' You know she loved that."

Allison looked at me. "You probably weren't too happy about that, were you?" she asked me with a knowing smile.

I shook my head. "No. And why did he single me out like that?" I wondered out loud. "I think Troy was pretty ticked, too. I mean, it really is his band and all. And there are three other members in Iron Wombat."

"He didn't look very happy," Katie pointed out.

"Hey, don't blame him," I replied. "Rick shouldn't have stolen Troy's spotlight by naming me. Troy's the band's front man. But at least Troy realized it wasn't my fault and didn't get mad at me."

"You were great, though, Randy, " Sabs said, giving me a big smile.

"Thanks, Sabs," I said, thinking how lucky I was to have such cool friends. "I don't think Stacy's ever going to forgive you, though,

Sabs," I went on, changing the subject.

"What are you talking about?" she asked, looking confused. "I know she wasn't very happy about having me there, but I wasn't playing in the band or anything."

"No, but you were dancing with Arizonna practically all night," Katie pointed out with a grin.

"It wasn't all night," Sabs protested. "I danced with Nick once."

"Once," I said to Katie and Al. "And that probably made Stacy even more upset. I mean, she thinks Nick is her personal property or something."

"That's true," Sabs admitted. "She was hanging all over him."

"Like clothes on a hanger," I agreed.

Al, Katie, and Sabs laughed. "What?" I asked, looking at all of them.

"Where do you get your expressions from?" Katie asked, and she cracked up again.

"Where do *I* get my expressions from?" I asked. "What about you guys? What was that one you said last week, Sabs? 'It's time to pay the piper'? What's that all about? Who's the piper? Is that like a midwest thing?"

"My mother says that all the time," Sabs told me. "You've never heard that before?"

"Definitely not," I stated. "But I like it!"

"You know, I wonder how long a conversation we could have if we only talked in clichés like these," Al mused out loud. It was a typical Allison thought. She wants to be a writer and she's always thinking in these literary ways. Once she wanted to say stuff only in alliterations — you know, when every word begins with the same letter. It was fabulously fantastically fun.

"'Only time will tell,'" Katie said, with a grin at me.

"Hey, 'I'm so hungry, I could eat a horse,'" I added as I scrambled out of my sleeping bag, stood up, and headed for the stairs. Sabs has the coolest room — it's in the attic. All the walls are sloped and stuff, and it's really big. I guess that's one of the pluses of being the only girl in the family. She gets her own room. Being an only child, I can't imagine having four brothers. Even though Sabrina's oldest brother is away at school, that still leaves four kids and two parents at home. I don't know if I'd like having so many people around me all the time.

Anyway, everyone else must have been hungry, too, because they all got out of their sleeping bags and grabbed a robe. We clattered down two flights of stairs to the kitchen. Sabs moaned as soon as she stepped into the room and saw the pile of dirty dishes in the sink.

"Sam!" she exclaimed. "'Am I my brother's keeper?'" She grinned at all of us.

"Come on, Sabs," Katie said, trying to keep the smile off her face. "He's 'more fun than a barrelful of monkeys.'"

"But Mom talked to him about cleaning up after himself," Sabs complained. I was about to say something because I thought she had forgotten to tack a cliché on the end, when she continued: "Oh, well. You know how that is. 'In one ear, and out the other.'"

"Don't worry, Sabs," Al added. "'What goes around comes around.'"

We all cracked up.

"Enough!" I exclaimed when I could speak again. I clutched my side — I was laughing so hard, I got a stitch. "I can't take it anymore. Let's talk normal again. It's much easier."

"I don't know, Randy," Al said, winking at me. "'The grass is always greener on the other side of the fence.'" I threw a dish towel at her.

"I think I want an omelette this morning," I said, opening Sabs's refrigerator.

"Sounds good," Katie agreed. "Are you going to cook?"

"Sure," I replied. I love to cook. It's probably a good thing, too. M doesn't cook too much. It's not that she can't cook. In fact, she's great when she puts her mind to it, but she just doesn't like to take the time. We'd practically live on Chinese takeout if I didn't get into cooking sometimes.

"Great!" Sabs exclaimed. "I want ham and cheese in mine."

"I want onions, too," Katie added.

"Al?" I asked, waving a spatula at her. "What do you want?"

"How about green peppers?" she asked.

"Cool deal," I replied. "Who's making the toast?"

"I can handle that," Sabs said, pulling out a loaf of bread from the bread box. Katie started making orange juice, and Allison got out plates and silverware and stuff.

The back door suddenly swung open and Sam and his friends Nick, Jason, and Arizonna came bursting in.

"Psych!" Sam exclaimed. "We're just in time for breakfast."

"You had breakfast already!" Sabs retorted, pointing to the dirty dishes.

"For your information, that was Mark," Sam said. "I haven't eaten yet."

Sabs sighed. "Brothers!" she exclaimed.

"What are we having?" Nick asked, taking a swig of the orange juice Katie had just finished making.

"We?" I asked, arching an eyebrow.

"R.Z.," Zone began. "You wouldn't like make us starve, would you? Be a babe."

"Be a babe?" I asked Allison. "What do you think?"

"Well, we don't want them wasting away before our very eyes," Al replied with a smile. "Let's feed the starving boys."

"Cool deal!" Nick exclaimed. "Are we having those great home fries you made a couple of weeks ago, too?"

"Only if you peel the potatoes," I shot back.

"What?" Sam asked. "You want us to work for our breakfast? I don't know what to think about this."

"Then don't think about it," Sabs said, handing him the bag of potatoes and the peeler. "Just go to it."

"Me?" Sam wanted to know. "Why me? Why not Jason?" He handed the peeler to Jason.

"Hey, don't worry about it," I said, opening the silverware drawer. I pulled out three more peelers and handed them over. "There's more where that came from. You can all work. I wouldn't want anyone to feel left out or anything."

"You guys kicked last night, Randy," Jason said as he sat down and started peeling. Even though Jason is the quietest of Sam's friends, he is definitely the best sport.

"Thanks, Jason," I replied. "It was okay, I guess. I definitely thought we did better at the Roadhouse, though. I just wasn't pumped enough."

"Well, what did that agent dude, Stacy's uncle, think?" Zone asked. "He's the one who matters, right?"

We're in trouble if he's the one that really matters, I thought to myself. But I didn't say anything. Why make a big deal out of it?

"Iron Wombat's going to cut a demo!" Sabs exclaimed. "Isn't that cool?"

"Awesome!" Zone agreed. "Troy must be very psyched. When?"

"Next week," I replied, trying not to think about it. I didn't really know how to tell Troy that I didn't want to do it.

"Ohmygosh!" Sam exclaimed, sounding just like Sabs. "I can say I knew you when after you hit the cover of *Rolling Stone*. Maybe they'll even interview me."

"That's getting just a little ahead of things, isn't it?" I asked with a grin. "I mean, zillions of bands cut demos. Very few of those actually cut albums."

"But still," Sam protested. "Let me think of what I can reveal to *Rolling Stone*. I'll tell them all about your kamikaze skateboarding. Or maybe I'll tell them how you made us peel potatoes until our fingers fell off."

"Wait until we're on the charts, okay?" I teased. "On the top of the charts."

"What song are you going to do on your demo?" Nick wanted to know. "'Fade Out'?"

"I guess so," I replied with a shrug. "I mean, it's our best. Well, I think so, anyway."

"Has nothing to do with the fact that you wrote the lyrics, right?" Zone asked.

"That's right," I agreed. "That has nothing to do with it. It's totally an objective decision. So, how are those potatoes doing?"

Sam chucked the potatoes at me one at a time. I chopped them up and dropped them in a frying pan with some onions. This was the way they made them at my favorite diner in New York.

After we finished breakfast, I sat back in my chair. "I'll never eat again," I moaned. "I'm going to explode."

"You always say that," Sabs pointed out.

"That's because I always mean it," I replied.

"Well, since we made breakfast, guess who gets to clean up?" Katie asked, looking at the guys.

"What?" Sam retorted, sounding shocked. "We peeled the potatoes."

"Please," Sabs said, throwing a dish towel at her brother. "You're on KP today, anyway."

The Wellses don't believe in division of labor according to sex. Everyone has to do everything. In other words, everyone has to take a turn on kitchen patrol — even Mr. Wells.

And everyone has to take turns cutting the lawn — even Sabs. There's no such thing as women's work and men's work. I think that is the way to run a household. I used to hate going to my Uncle Oliver's on Long Island when we still lived in New York. His wife, my Aunt Edith, did everything around the house. He would just sit there as she cleared the table and washed the dishes. I never saw him even get one thing out of the refrigerator. I never would have stood for that. This is the nineties.

"So, like, what's going on today?" Zone asked as he headed toward the sink.

"I don't know," Sabs admitted. "We hadn't really thought about it. Do you have to practice today, Randy?"

"Not if Troy doesn't know where I am," I replied with a grin. "I need a break, anyway. Let's escape. I never thought I'd get sick of my drums, but I definitely need to get away from them."

Just saying that out loud suddenly made me feel a whole lot better. I just could not face another second of practice — otherwise, I felt as if I'd never want to play again. And I couldn't let that happen.

Chapter Seven

"This is cool," Alton said for about the twentieth time. "This is very cool."

It was Thursday afternoon and we were at J & G Recording Studios in downtown Minneapolis, waiting for Slick Rick. After my Sunday of playing hooky, I'd gone back to practicing with the band for the next four days. Finally the big day had arrived. We were about to cut a demo. Even I was excited — a little. But Slick was about twenty minutes late. And we were all getting more and more tense as the seconds ticked by.

"How's everyone doing?" Troy asked as he paced back and forth. "Are you all pumped?"

"I was twenty minutes ago," I muttered, banging my drumsticks on my kneecap. I hate waiting for anything.

Five minutes later, Slick breezed in. Todayhe was wearing black pleated pants, a white tab-collar shirt, and little black Italian shoes with tassels. I could tell he really thought he was something.

"Hi, kids," he said, not even taking off his sunglasses. Of course, there was no apology for keeping us waiting for almost half an hour. I hadn't really expected one from him, but still.

"Hi, Rick," Troy replied, shaking his hand. "We're all set."

"Fabulous," Slick said, swinging to look at me. "Hey, Randy, how's it going? What's 'Randy' stand for, anyway?"

"Randy," I replied flatly. I happen to hate my real name, Rowena. I don't know what my parents were thinking when they named me. No one calls me Rowena — except a teacher or two. I usually won't answer to it.

Rick's eyebrows lifted over the tops of his sunglasses. "Really?" he said to no one in particular. "I had hoped it would be something a little more feminine."

What did it matter, I wondered. Suddenly I wasn't feeling very comfortable anymore. Why was it such a big deal to this guy that I was a girl who plays the drums? I had talked to D earlier in the week and he was going to check on Slick for me — you know, find out what he could about him. D did say that Oakland Records is a very respected label. But D also told me not to sign a thing until he looked it over. I was actually pretty glad he had said that. The more I saw of Slick Rick, the more nervous I was getting.

"Well, come on, kids," Rick went on. "We're in Studio C."

"Kids?" Alton asked me in a low voice as we followed Slick down the hall.

Slick had told us not to cart our equipment down. He said that he was going to hook us up. I felt weird walking to a gig with just my drumsticks.

Pushing open a door marked "C," Slick flipped on the light switch and waited until we were all inside. We were standing in the control room, with the board and recording equipment. Through the big glass wall I could see the actual playing studio. A drum set, keyboard, and two guitars were waiting.

"Cool deal," Troy exclaimed.

Slick grinned at us. "This is it, kids," he said in a patronizing tone. "The big time. I'm going to go scavenge up an engineer. Why don't you head on in and warm up?"

After Slick left, we silently filed into the studio. Even though I hadn't been looking forward to this, I still felt a little thrill — a surge of excitement. This really was the big time. Walking over to the drum set, I twirled my sticks. None of us were looking at each other, I noticed. I think everyone was kind of awed by the place.

"Wow!" Alton exclaimed, gingerly picking up the bass guitar. "This is beautiful!" He strapped it on and pulled a turquoise pick out of his pocket. Lightly running it down the strings, Alton sighed. "Unbelievable!"

I sat down at the stool behind the drums and just stared at them. This was a major set — nothing like my battered drums at home. So this was what the big time was like. There were definitely some things about it I could get used to real fast.

Jim walked around, touching every piece of equipment. Troy just picked up a pair of earphones and put them on. He stood at the lead mike and stared through the glass wall to the control room. I wondered what he was thinking.

I was glad Slick had left. It probably wouldn't have been cool for him to see us looking like a bunch of awestruck kids. He already thought we were amateurs. I didn't want to do anything to prove him right.

Running my sticks over the drums, I grinned at the sound. Suddenly I felt ready to rock. These drums were awesome, and the sound in the room was incredible. It was certainly a far cry from the garage behind Troy's house. We could do some serious jamming here.

"Let's rock the house!" I exclaimed to the rest of Iron Wombat.

Troy spun around and grinned at me. "It's not so painful, is it?" he asked. I guess he knows me better than I think. I'd really thought I was hiding my true feelings about this demo pretty well. Apparently I was wrong.

"Do you think they'd notice if I left with this drum set?" I asked.

"Nah," Alton replied. "Just pop it in your back pocket or something."

We all laughed, and I could feel the tension in the room ease a little.

"All right, kids," the speaker on the wall

suddenly said. Startled, I looked through the glass wall and saw Slick standing there. A big, balding guy with a long beard and mustache was sitting in front of the board. "This is Clyde."

We all waved. Clyde just looked bored.

"I want you to do that song, what's it called?" Slick continued.

"'Fade Out,'" Troy replied quickly.

"Right," Slick replied. "And make sure you do that guitar and drum duel thing in the beginning."

I shot a glance at Troy. He hadn't mentioned that to me, maybe because he had known that I really wouldn't want to do it.

. "That's not part of the song," I protested.

"Well, it's what I want," Slick replied, apparently not caring about the song.

Sighing, I glared at Troy. He stared back.

"Unless, of course, you just can't do it," Slick continued, patting his gelled, shellacked hair. Idly, I wondered if his hair would crack, because it looked so stiff.

"No problem," Troy said quickly, with another look at me.

"I'm up for it," I added, standing up to

adjust the height of my stool.

"Good," Slick announced. "I didn't want you to get all girlie on me now."

My head snapped up. *Girlie?* What was that supposed to mean? Even though he wasn't Stacy's blood relative, I could definitely see some similarities.

"All right, when you're ready," Slick continued.

"Put a lid on it," Troy said to me quietly. I hadn't even noticed him sliding up to me. "Don't lose it, Z. I can't afford to blow this."

Glaring at him, I sat back down on my stool. "Maybe if you put half as much effort into English as you do to dealing with Slick Rick, this whole demo thing wouldn't be such a big-time deal. And I wouldn't have to sit here listening to 'girlie' cracks," I said.

"What?" Troy asked, his eyes narrowing. "How did you hear about English? I never told you."

"Well, let's just say I heard it somewhere," I replied, looking away quickly.

"Are you ready, kids?" Slick asked, sounding impatient. "I've got another group coming in an hour. We don't have all day."

Shooting me one more glare, Troy stalked back to his guitar. After he strapped it on, he gave Slick the thumbs-up. Then he looked at me, as if daring me to start something major.

I wasn't going to. I mean, I was just going to do my thing — just the way I had at Stacy's party. But the drums were too beautiful, the sound was too good, and I was just too mad at Troy and good ole Slick. As soon as my stick hit the drum, the whole scene started to fade. I knew then, in some part of my mind, that in spite of the way I felt about what we were doing, we were going to seriously jam today.

And we did. I didn't have to see Slick's face to know that we had. I just knew it. Of course, Slick being Slick, he made us do like ten cuts of it. But that first jam was the most serious.

After about an hour, Slick cut us off and told us to wrap it up. Alton reluctantly unstrapped the guitar and put it back on the stand. He looked as if he was walking away from his girl-friend or something, the way he kept looking back at that guitar. Jim took a last look around at all the equipment, and then he followed Alton into the control room.

Troy put his guitar down and walked back

to me. "Thanks," he said softly. "You did good."

"You're weren't too bad yourself," I replied with a grin. "A little late on that second take, but not too shabby."

"Late!" Troy exclaimed, smiling back at me. "You were early, babe."

Slick blew into the mike impatiently. "Let's go, people," he announced. "We've got to vacate."

"That man is on the edge," I muttered as I filed out after Troy. I hated to leave those drums behind. But I had a feeling a set like that was definitely in my future, so I was only saying "see you later" to them and not "goodbye."

Clyde was already in the midst of making some edits on all those takes we had done. I was right about the first drum/guitar duel — Clyde was using that. Jim sat down next to him, and raptly watched him work. I could get into it. It was kind of neat to keep hearing the sound of Iron Wombat fill the room.

"So, I'll be getting in touch," Slick said as he sat down and put his feet up on a table in the center of the room. "And when Clyde is finished editing, I'll send you a copy."

"Cool deal," Troy replied, his eyes never leaving Clyde.

"Like, that's it," Slick continued. "Come on, kids, I've got another group coming in any sec. Time to clear out."

This dude was definitely short on manners.

"Right," Troy said, tearing his eyes away and backing toward the door. Jim lingered in the chair next to Clyde. They actually had a quasi-conversation going. Unbelievable. Was treble level that intriguing a topic of discussion?

Troy opened the door and motioned to us to follow. I was the last one heading out.

"Oh, Randy," Slick said casually. "Hang for a minute?"

I glanced at Troy. I really didn't want to spend even one more second with Slick, but Troy was throwing me one of those pleading looks again.

"We'll wait right out here," Troy said, pointing to the hallway.

"Shut the door after you, would you?" Slick asked him, brushing his nails on the palm of his other hand.

Troy raised his eyebrows at me, but shut the door. I gripped my drumsticks tightly and turned toward Slick.

"Have a seat, babe," he said, gesturing to the empty chair across from him with his foot.

"I'd rather stand," I replied defiantly. I didn't like this dude, and no matter what Troy said, I wasn't about to pretend that I did.

Slick laughed. "You've got a great attitude," he said, touching his shellacked head. Any moment I expected broken pieces of hair to start falling to the floor.

I didn't say anything.

"Where you from, anyway?" he continued.

"New York," I replied shortly.

"Of course," he said. "Randy Zak from New York. Zak. Hey, are you any relation to Peter Zak, the director?"

"He's my father," I answered just as shortly.

"Talented guy," he replied. "We worked with him on a video a while back. He's definitely good."

He wasn't going to get an argument from me. But if Slick thought that he could change the way I felt about him by complimenting my dad, he was sadly mistaken.

"So, what are you doing here in Middle Nowhere, U.S.A.?" Slick asked.

"I like Acorn Falls," I protested. Who was he to insult my town?

"Right," Slick replied, as if he didn't believe me.

I tapped my foot impatiently, waiting for him to get to the point. I really wasn't in the mood to chat about where I lived. Besides, that was none of his business.

"Anyway, Randy," Slick went on, swinging his feet onto the floor and sitting up a little straighter. "Are you sure your name doesn't stand for something else?"

I just fixed him with a stony glare.

"No matter," he said with a wave of his hand. "We could always make something up."

"What are you talking about?" I asked, cutting right to it. Enough was enough.

"Listen, Iron Wombat is a pretty decent little band," Slick said.

Little band? I was glad Troy was standing out in the hall and couldn't hear this. I didn't think he'd take too well to what Slick was saying or the really condescending way he was saying it.

"But decent little bands are a dime a dozen," Slick continued, with another pat to his head.

"What's your point?" I asked, wondering what was coming next.

"A girl drummer is another thing," he replied. "And you're even talented."

"So?" I asked.

"That attitude is perfect," Slick said with a chuckle. "And I think I could take you all the way."

All the way where? I wondered. I didn't want to go even an inch farther with this guy. "What do you mean?" I asked again.

"You've got to go solo," Slick said, picking up a pencil and tapping it on the table. "That band is just extra baggage for you. I could promote you as the new young Buddy Rich, girl-style."

Girl-style? Where did this guy get his expressions from? His vocabulary definitely needed some work.

"Listen," I replied shortly. "We're a band. You know, all four of us are like a package. A band. Either you want all of us, or you don't."

"Is that the way you want to play this?" he

asked, arching his eyebrows at me.

I nodded.

"Your loyalty to your band is admirable," Slick said. "But it's not going to get you anywhere. I think you're making a really hasty choice. Maybe you want to think about it."

"And maybe I don't," I shot back. This guy was a real helmet head.

"Hey, it's no skin off my nose," Slick said, throwing up his hands. "It's your career."

"That's right," I agreed. "It's my career and my decision. And I've decided that I'm going to stick with my friends and our 'decent little band.' And I've also decided that I don't want to have anything to do with you. I'm going all the way to the top, but there's no way I'm going to let you ride on my train to success!"

His mouth dropped open, as if he wasn't used to people talking to him like that. He probably wasn't too used to being rejected either. And I was definitely doing that.

I heard a giggle and turned toward the sound. Clyde grinned at me and let out another giggle. What a strange sound for such a big man.

"Stay cool, Clyde," I said, spinning toward

the door. I just wanted to get out of there.

Slick Rick held up two fingers in a peace sign. "See you around," he replied.

I turned and glared at him. "Count on it," I said slowly. Then I opened the door and stepped out into the hallway. I felt as if I was stepping out of the frying pan and into the fire. Now that I was finished with Mr. Slick, I was going to have come up with something to tell Troy. I didn't know how to tell him Slick didn't want Iron Wombat. I had a feeling it wouldn't go over very well.

Chapter Eight

Sabrina calls Randy.

RANDY: Talk to me.

SABRINA: Randy? It's Sabs. How'd the demo session go? You were so quiet in school today I thought something went wrong.

RANDY: Well, something did kind of go wrong. We went and cut the demo yesterday.

SABRINA: That's great, so what's the problem?

RANDY: The problem is that the agent didn't want the band.

SABRINA: Hey, I'm sorry. But you guys are just getting started, and there are tons of agents out there.

RANDY: I know, I know. But the problem is that this agent just wanted to sign me — only me.

Sabrina whistles.

SABRINA: Wow! That's hard. So what are you going to do?

RANDY: I told him to forget it.

SABRINA: Good for you! I told you I didn't like that guy. What do you call him — Slicky Ricky?

Randy laughs.

RANDY: Just Slick Rick. But I have another problem. I haven't told the rest of the band about what Rick said.

SABRINA: When are you going to tell them?

RANDY: I don't know. And on top of it all, I don't even know *how* to tell them. I mean, Troy was so incredibly into this whole thing. He really wanted to show his parents how serious he is about music.

SABRINA: Hmm, why didn't Slick Rick want Iron Wombat? You guys are great.

RANDY: Yeah. Well, Slick Rick only wanted me because I'm a girl.

SABRINA: Huh?

RANDY: You know, a girl drummer. I think he wanted to turn me into a publicity stunt.

SABRINA: Well, maybe that's what you can tell Troy. Maybe it will make him feel better.

RANDY: I don't know, Sabs. I'm just afraid that Troy will only hear that he wasn't wanted and I was.

SABRINA: You're probably right.

RANDY: I hope I'm wrong.

SABRINA: Why don't you call Al. She's good at figuring out what to say.

RANDY: Yeah, I was thinking about that.

SABRINA: Go ahead. Listen, call me back if you want to talk some more.

RANDY: Hey, thanks, Sabs, I will. *Ciao*.

SABRINA: Talk to you later.

Randy calls Allison.

ALLISON: Cloud residence. Allison speaking.

RANDY: Hi, Al. It's me.

ALLISON: Hey, Randy. How are you?

RANDY: I'm okay. How's your mom doing? How's the baby coming along?

ALLISON: Well, it's early yet. Nothing much

is happening. I don't think my mom feels all that great, though. Sometimes she looks almost green.

RANDY: Really? Oh, well, I bet you can't wait until it's born.

ALLISON: Yeah, but it's going to be a while yet. Hey, how are you?

RANDY: I'm okay, I guess, but I do have things on my mind.

ALLISON: I figured. Is it about Iron Wombat and the demo?

RANDY: Bull's-eye! Al, you are amazing.

ALLISON: Not really. What's up?

RANDY: Well, Slick didn't want Iron Wombat. He only wanted me for, and I quote, "the new young Buddy Rich — girl-style."

ALLISON: Girl-style? Yuk.

RANDY: You got it. I think he's such a weirdo!

ALLISON: So what did you tell him?

RANDY: No, of course.

ALLISON: But I thought you always wanted to be a solo drummer, just like Buddy Rich.

RANDY: I did. I mean, I do. But I'm not a solo drummer now. I'm part of a band. I would be lower than a snake to take any deal without them.

ALLISON: I see. So how did Troy take the news?

RANDY: Well, that's just it. I haven't really told him yet. I don't even know what to say to him.

ALLISON: I think you should just tell him the truth.

RANDY: I'm going to. I just don't know how to say it. I guess I should just say it, right?

ALLISON: Right. And why don't you suggest that he gets extra help in English.

RANDY: Oh, yeah, right. I'm sure he'll listen to that from me.

ALLISON: Well, *you* could help him, you know.

RANDY: Me?

ALLISON: Sure. He's in ninth grade, right? Well, that probably means his problem is the writing portfolio.

RANDY: How could I help him? You're the
            one who wants to be a writer.

ALLISON: And you're the one who writes
            songs — with him.

RANDY: Oh. That's true. Hey, thanks for
            the advice, Al. I should have
            talked to you earlier. You always
            know what to do.

ALLISON: Randy, the most important thing
            is to let Troy know about all of
            this as soon as possible.

RANDY: All right. I'm going to try and call
            Troy now.

ALLISON: Good luck.

RANDY: Thanks, Al.

ALLISON: No problemo.

Randy laughs.

RANDY: I'm really rubbing off on you, Al.
            Catch ya on the rebound.

ALLISON: Good night.

Chapter Nine

"Hi, Troy," I said as he opened his front door. It was the next morning, and I had gone over to Troy's first thing. After hanging up from Al the day before, I really did some thinking. And one of the things I'd decided was that this kind of thing needed a personal visit, not a phone call. So I got up first thing and went over to Troy's. I didn't want to put it off any longer.

"R.Z.!" Troy exclaimed, still looking sleepy. "What's the word? You're really up at the break of dawn."

"It's not that early," I protested. "Do you want me to come back later?"

"No, no," Troy replied, rubbing his eyes. "Come on in. Oh, better yet, why don't we go out back?"

He stepped out onto the porch and I followed him around to the back of his house. The Tanners have this old separate garage building that they never use since they put up a carport. Troy cleaned it out, and Iron Wombat uses it for practices.

Troy threw himself onto an old easy chair and put his feet up on a milk crate. I was too keyed up to sit and started pacing around the garage. I ran my fingers over the cymbal of my drum set instead.

"What's up? You look on edge," Troy said, and then yawned.

"Well . . ." I began and then stopped. Taking a deep breath, I told myself to get it over with.

"You know how Rick asked me to stay in the control room after you guys left?" I asked.

"Yeah," Troy responded. "You said he wanted to talk about your father or something."

"Well, that wasn't really true," I admitted. "I mean, it was in a way. We did talk about D. But what Rick really wanted to do was offer me a record deal."

"Seriously!" Troy exclaimed, suddenly looking very awake. "That is too cool! Why didn't you say anything? You know how key this all is. This is great! We're going to be awesome! I always knew it! Wait until I tell my parents!"

Oops, I thought. He definitely had the wrong idea. "Me, Troy," I said as soon as I could get a word in edgewise. "Me. Not Iron Wombat."

Troy stopped mid-whoop. "What?" he asked.

"Slick offered me a record deal," I repeated. "He thought a solo girl drummer was a great angle."

"Solo?" Troy wanted to know. His eyes narrowed slightly.

"Right," I replied. "That's what he said."

Troy got really quiet. The silence stretched out for what felt like an eternity. I didn't know what to say and kept wishing he'd just get mad or something. But he just sat there, staring straight ahead. Not like Troy at all.

"So, what did you tell him?" Troy asked finally.

Troy actually thought I took the deal. I didn't believe it!

"What do you think I told him?" I wanted to know.

"I don't know," Troy shot back. "That's why I asked you."

"Some faith," I muttered.

"What?" Troy asked, jumping to his feet. Then he started pacing around the garage. There we were, pacing around the garage in opposite directions.

"I told him no!" I yelled.

"What?" Troy asked again, this time sounding shocked. "You did?"

"Yeah," I admitted a little more quietly. "And then I told him that I wasn't going to let him ride on my train to success."

"You didn't!" Troy said.

"I did," I said defiantly, thinking he was mad about that.

"That was definitely cool," Troy replied, grinning at me.

"I was just so ticked at Slick," I admitted. "I couldn't help it."

"Slick?" Troy asked, laughing. "I love it! He's definitely a slick dude."

"Seriously," I replied. "He was a major phony. I'm glad he didn't offer us anything. I wouldn't want to make him rich."

"And we would make someone rich, right?" Troy asked, sitting down on the stool behind my drum set. He picked up a pair of sticks that I keep there just in case I forget my favorite ones. Experimentally, he tapped the snare drum a few times.

"Not too shabby," I complimented him. "Soon you'll be a one-man band."

"No way," he replied. "We're a four-man band all the way."

"Four-man?" I asked, teasing him.

"Uh, four-member," he shot back. "You know, Randy, if Rick had offered just me a deal, I don't know what I would have done. I would like to say that I definitely would have turned him down, but I don't know if I could have."

"You would have," I stated firmly. "You don't think so, now. But I bet in the same situation you would have told him the same thing I did."

"I don't know," Troy replied.

I nodded.

"I don't think I would ever tell someone that they couldn't ride on my train to success," Troy said, cracking up. "In fact, I don't think it would have even occurred to me to say that."

"Oh, you're cruising for a bruising," I joked.

"I'm trembling with fright," he teased back.

Suddenly he dropped the drumsticks and stood up again. "Now, what am I going to do?"

he asked quietly.

"About your parents?" I wanted to know.

"Right," he replied. "Now, they're going to get on me about my grades again."

"Well, why don't you just do better in school?" I suggested. "What's the big deal?"

"It's writing!" Troy exclaimed. "You know how I write. You've heard my songs. You said yourself that my lyrics were as exciting as a limp dishrag. How am I going to fill up a writing portfolio with a wet dishrag? I hate writing essays."

"Why don't you do something different?" I suggested. "That's the whole point, right? You don't have to write essays, do you?"

"No," he replied. "But what else could I do?"

"Well, I don't know," I admitted.

"Some big help you are," he said.

"Hey," I protested. "I remember once in my old school back in New York, we had to write letters."

"Letters?" Troy asked, sounding confused.

"Yeah," I replied. "You know, writing letters to somebody."

"Why would I want to write anybody?"

Troy wanted to know. "And what would I say?"

"Well, we had to pretend that we were somewhere else, and we were writing someone back home," I answered.

"But who would I write to, and where would I be?" Troy asked.

I laughed. "What am I, the answer bank? What's your favorite thing to do?"

"Play, of course," Troy replied quickly.

"So, why don't you pretend that you're out in like L.A. or something, or New York, and you've made it," I suggested.

Troy was silent for a moment. Then he said, "I could do that."

"Sure you could," I replied. "And you could be writing to someone back here in Acorn Falls, you know, describing what it's like and everything."

"I could definitely do that," Troy said again, sounding excited. "I could really get into this."

"Cool deal," I said with a grin. "You better get into it now so you pass English, right?"

"Okay, okay, I'll try it," Troy replied with a laugh. "I'd better do something about my English grade, and at this point I'm willing to try anything. Uh, Randy, remember how you were shocked when I gave you a compliment?"

"How could I forget that famous moment," I said, shaking my head.

"Well, hold on to your boots because here's another one. Randy, you're the greatest. I'll never forget what you said to Slick Rick and . . . what you did for Iron Wombat," Troy said seriously.

We stared at each other for a few seconds and we cracked up.

"Hey, Tanner, what is this? One of those special coffee moments, like they have on TV?" I asked, trying to lighten things up.

"Well, don't go getting all *girlie* on me, *Zakster*, it's just a compliment — don't get used to them."

"Girlie! Did you call me 'girlie'? Why you . . . you . . . ."

"Friend," Troy said quietly. And we both just smiled.

"So, what are you up to today?" Troy asked, changing the subject. "I was thinking about having a practice."

"No way!" I said firmly. "I'm going to hang out with my friends." I had to tell them how right they had been about being straight with Troy. As usual, they had given me the best advice I could get. But I guess that's what best friends are all about.

Don't miss
GIRL TALK #19
FAMILY AFFAIR

I woke up with a start at the sound of my alarm buzzing loudly. I reached over to the night table next to my bed and pressed the top of the clock until the buzzing stopped.

It was six-forty-five. Good. I probably had time to get into the shower before everyone else. I looked out my bedroom window and frowned at the cold Minnesota rain. I wished it was cold enough to snow. Then I could go ice-skating with my best friends Sabrina, Allison, and Randy.

Then I remembered it was Monday morning and a school day. I turned away from the window with a sigh. Since it was Monday morning, I didn't have time to worry about the rain outside. I had to get into the shower quickly before someone else did, or I'd be late for school.

I couldn't believe that it had only been a month since my mom had remarried. It was even harder to believe that only two weeks ago, my mom's new husband, Jean-Paul Beauvais, and his son Michel, had moved in with us.

Now our house was totally packed! The basement was stuffed with most of the Beauvaises' furniture. Michel was sleeping in the guest room but the family room had thousands of cardboard boxes and wooden crates on the floor. I couldn't watch TV without having to move something out of my way. But the worst of it was the bathroom situation. Five people living in a house with only one bathroom was a real pain.

Suddenly I heard my sister Emily open her bedroom door. Knowing Emily, I had to move fast or I'd have to wait ages to get into the bathroom.! I grabbed my pink bathrobe and ran into the hall. Just as I got to the door of the bathroom, Emily jumped in front of me.

"Relax, Katherine. I just need the hair dryer," my sister said. I hate it when she calls me Katherine! Emily leaned over and grabbed the hair dryer from the cabinet under the sink. Then she turned and disappeared into her bedroom. When she left, I closed the bathroom door tightly and let out a long breath of air.

Now it was my turn for a long hot shower. I turned on the faucet and stepped into the shower. I screamed the second the icy water hit me. I shivered and spun the knobs again. This was the third time in two weeks that there was no hot water. Everyone else must have taken their showers and used up all the hot water. I made up my mind right then and there that if I was going to survive in this family, I was going to have to get up at least an hour earlier every morning — probably for the rest of my life!

Look for these titles in the
GIRL TALK series

LOOK FOR THE GIRL TALK SERIES!
IN A STORE NEAR YOU!

TALK BACK!

TELL US WHAT YOU THINK ABOUT GIRL TALK

Name _Bootsie King_

Address _212 Manassas Dr_

City _Manassas_ State _VA_ Zip _22111_

Birthday Day _26_ Mo. _7_ Year _81_

Telephone Number _(703) 361-5420_

1) On a scale of 1 (The Pits) to 5 (The Max),
how would you rate Girl Talk? Circle One:

1   2   3   4   (5)

2) What do you like most about Girl Talk?

___Characters ✓Situations___Telephone Talk

Other _____

3) Who is your favorite character? Circle One:

(Sabrina)   Katie   Randy

Allison   Stacy   Other

4) Who is your least favorite character?

_____ Stacy _____

5) What do you want to read about in Girl Talk?

_____

_____

Send completed form to :
Western Publishing Company, Inc.
1220 Mound Avenue Mail Station #85
Racine, Wisconsin 53404